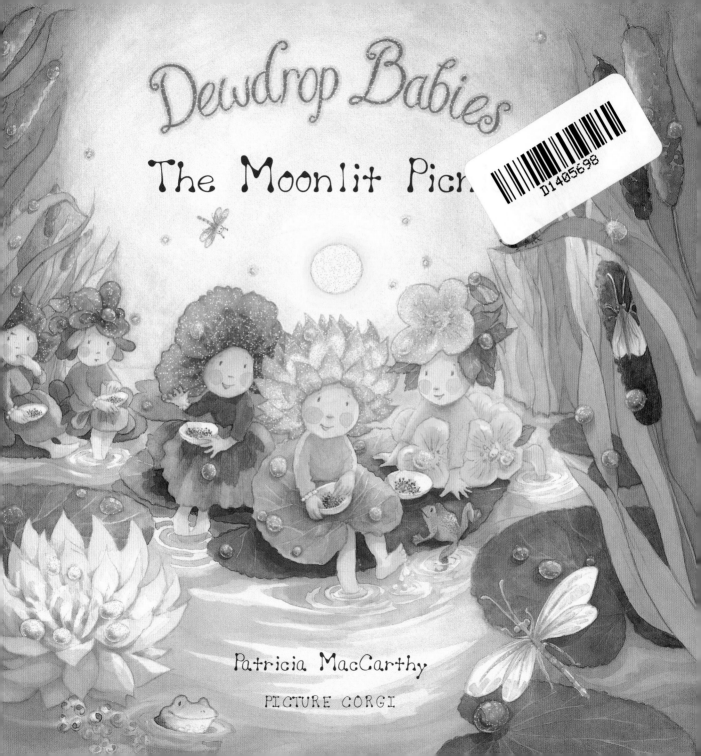

Dewdrop Babies

The Moonlit Picnic

Patricia MacCarthy

PICTURE CORGI

It's night-time, the glow-worms have turned off their lights, and the Dewdrop Babies are tucked up in their cosy petal beds in the underground palace.

But one of the Babies is wide awake . . .

Naughty Buttercup can't even think about sleeping.
She wants to have some fun!

"Wake up, Poppy," she whispers in her friend's ear.
"Let's go and see Waterlily. Her lily flower only
opens at night. She'll be at the lake now!"

"Oooh yes" Poppy squeaks. "We can go boating – and have a moonlit picnic."

Poppy jumps out of bed. She's ready for adventure too!

Buttercup and Poppy dash to the palace storeroom.
They pile sunflower and poppy seeds into a basket.

"Ssssshh!"

"We must be quiet!" says Buttercup. "If Violet wakes up,
she'll try to stop us."

Fireflies light the way as Buttercup and Poppy skip along the tunnels and through the garden gate.

The garden is magical in the moonlight, and
the scent of the waterlily flower fills the air.

Buttercup and Poppy follow the scent down to the lake.

Waterlily is so pleased to see her friends!
"We can have a party!" she beams.
"But be careful not to fall in!"

Poppy and Buttercup don't want to be careful.
They leap onto the backs of two friendly pondskaters
and go whizzing across the water.

"Wheee! I feel dizzy!" laughs Buttercup.
Poppy's pondskater whizzes a bit too fast.

"Stop!"

But it is too late . . .

Poppy plops
into the lake.

She splashes about
in the water.

Then she sees something skimming across the lake
towards her.

It's Violet and
Bluebell, riding on
a waterboatman!

Violet scoops Poppy
out of the water

and Bluebell wraps her
up in a petal blanket.

"You saved me!" says Poppy. "How did you get here?"

"We followed your seed trail," explains Bluebell.

"We wanted to make sure you were OK!" adds Violet.

Buttercup gives Poppy a big hug, and Waterlily
has the perfect way to warm her up.

The five Dewdrop Babies bounce up and down
on the spider's web . . .

until the grumpy spider
tells them to trampoline somewhere else!

"Let's have our moonlit picnic now," suggests Waterlily.
They sit on giant lily leaves and munch on the yummy seeds.

Croak croak!

Croak croak!

The frogs come to see what's going on and the waterboatmen stand guard to make sure no one else falls in!

Croak croak!

Croak croak!

Suddenly, Buttercup turns white and bursts into tears.

"Oh NO! My dewdrop bracelet! It's gone!"

"You can't go back without it!"

The Dewdrop Babies dart to and fro,
hunting for Buttercup's sparkly bracelet.

"Where can it be?"

Just when Buttercup thinks she's lost her bracelet
for ever, Spider dangles down from his web, wearing
it on one of his legs!

"Oh, thank you, Spider!" beams Buttercup. "It
must have fallen off when we were all bouncing!"

"Perhaps it's time to go home now," says Bluebell.

"Before you get into any more trouble," Violet adds.

Buttercup and Poppy agree!

They all kiss Waterlily goodnight.

Then the moon moth flies the four tired Dewdrop Babies back to the palace.

Tucked up safely in bed again, Buttercup and Poppy decide that night-time adventures can be a bit too adventurous. Violet and Bluebell agree! And with that, they all fall fast asleep.

For Ian, Louise,
Oliver and Ruth

THE MOONLIT PICNIC
A PICTURE CORGI BOOK 978 0 552 55651 4

First published in Great Britain by Picture Corgi,
an imprint of Random House Children's Books
A Random House Group Company

This edition published 2008

1 3 5 7 9 10 8 6 4 2

Text copyright © Random House Children's Books, 2008
Illustrations copyright © Patricia MacCarthy, 2008
Concept © Random House Children's Books and Patricia MacCarthy, 2008
Text by Alison Ritchie
Design by Tracey Cunnell

The right of Patricia MacCarthy to be identified as the illustrator of this work
has been asserted in accordance with the Copyright, Designs and Patents Act 1988.

Picture Corgi Books are published by Random House Children's Books,
61-63 Uxbridge Road, London W5 5SA

www.dewdropbabies.com
www.rbooks.co.uk

Addresses for companies within The Random House Group Limited
can be found at: www.randomhouse.co.uk/offices.htm

THE RANDOM HOUSE GROUP Limited Reg. No. 954009

A CIP catalogue record for this book is available from the British Library.

Printed in China